A
COLOR SAMPLER

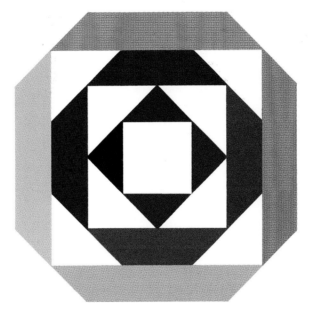

BY KATHLEEN WESTRAY

TICKNOR & FIELDS NEW YORK · 1993

Ticknor & Fields
A Houghton Mifflin company, 215 Park Avenue South,
New York, New York 10003.

Manufactured in the United States of America
Book design by Kathleen Westray
The text of this book is set in 14 pt. Sabon

HOR 10 9 8 7 6 5 4 3 2 1

Library of Congress Cataloging-in-Publication Data
Westray, Kathleen.
A color sampler / by Kathleen Westray.
p.   cm.
Summary: Discusses primary, secondary, and intermediate colors
and shows how color is affected by what is around it.
ISBN 0-395-65940-X
1. Color–Juvenile literature. 2. Colors–Juvenile literature.
[1. Color.] I. Title. QC495.5.W48 1993
535.6–dc20 93-19967 CIP AC

FOR MY MOTHER AND FATHER

with thanks to Norma Jean

RED

GREEN

RED-
VIOLET

BLUE-
GREEN

YELLOW

ORANGE

VIOLET

BLUE

YELLOW-
GREEN

COLOR is everywhere, and everything has color.
The variety of colors is endless,

and each color can look very different—
light or dark, fresh or faded, dazzling or muted.

Red, yellow, and blue are the three primary colors.

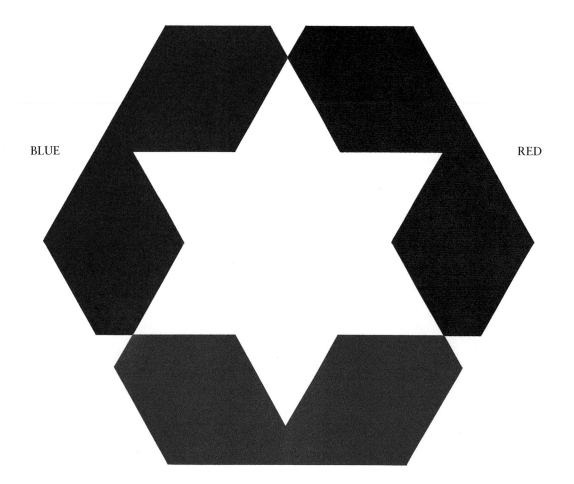

BLUE

RED

YELLOW

They are the only colors that cannot be made from any other colors, and all other colors are made with them.

Mixing two primary colors makes one of the three
secondary colors: orange, green, and violet.

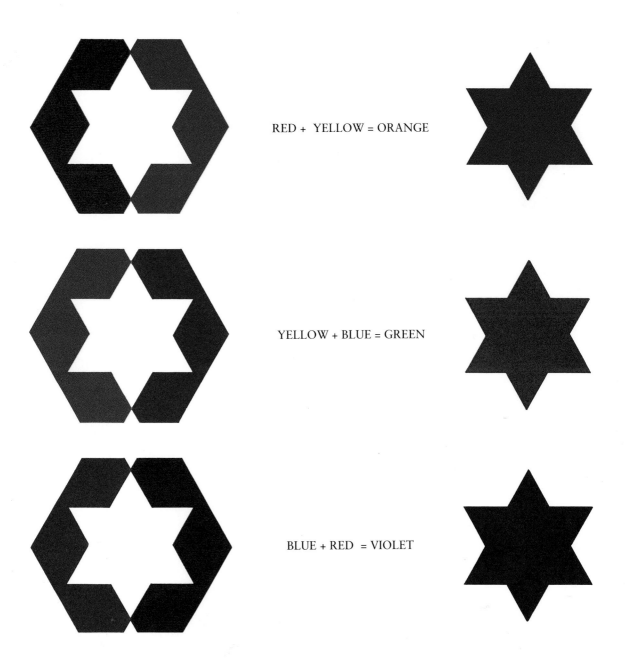

RED + YELLOW = ORANGE

YELLOW + BLUE = GREEN

BLUE + RED = VIOLET

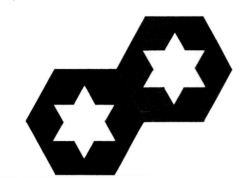

RED +
VIOLET =
RED-VIOLET

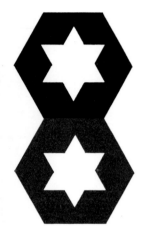

VIOLET +
BLUE =
BLUE-VIOLET

BLUE +
GREEN =
BLUE-GREEN

Mixing one of the primary colors with one of the

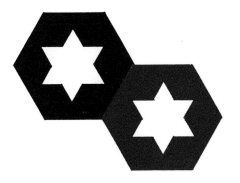

RED +
ORANGE =
RED-ORANGE

ORANGE +
YELLOW =
YELLOW-ORANGE

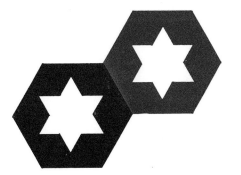

YELLOW +
GREEN =
YELLOW-GREEN

secondary colors makes one of six intermediate colors.

These twelve colors
(the primary, secondary,
and intermediate colors)
form the color wheel.
They always appear in
the same order. The
color wheel is a tool to
help people use and
understand color.

RED-VIOLET
(intermediate)

VIOLET
(secondary)

BLUE-VIOLET
(intermediate)

BLUE
(primary)

BLUE-GREEN
(intermediate)

GREEN
(secondary)

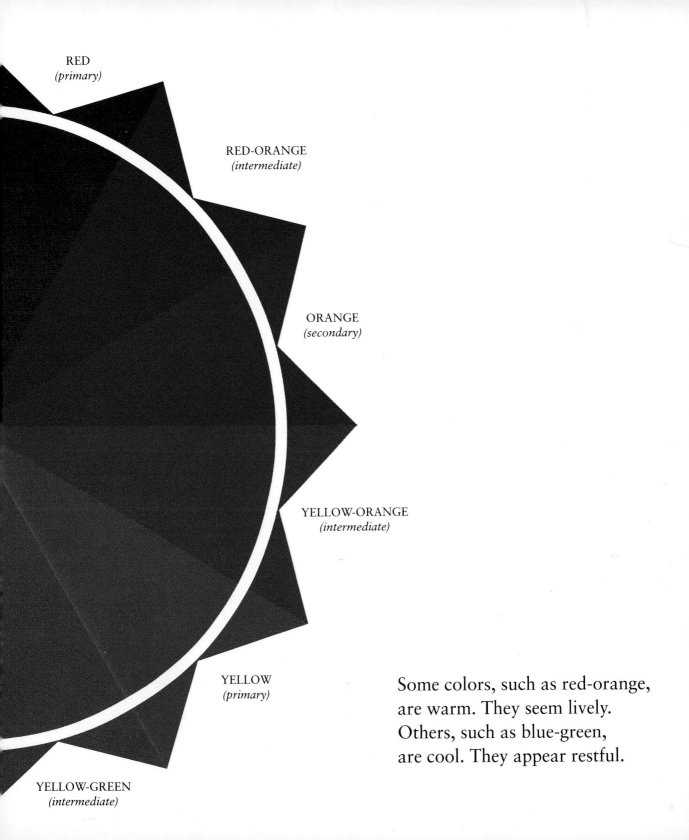

RED
(primary)

RED-ORANGE
(intermediate)

ORANGE
(secondary)

YELLOW-ORANGE
(intermediate)

YELLOW
(primary)

YELLOW-GREEN
(intermediate)

Some colors, such as red-orange, are warm. They seem lively. Others, such as blue-green, are cool. They appear restful.

From the twelve colors
on the color wheel,
hundreds of other
colors can be made.

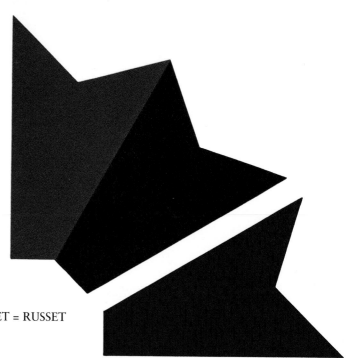

ORANGE + VIOLET = RUSSET

GREEN + ORANGE = CITRON

VIOLET + GREEN = OLIVE

RED-ORANGE + BLUE-GREEN = BROWN

Black and white are also colors.

Mixing red, yellow, and blue is
the simplest way of making black.

Mixing black and white makes gray.
More black than white makes dark gray.
More white than black makes light gray.

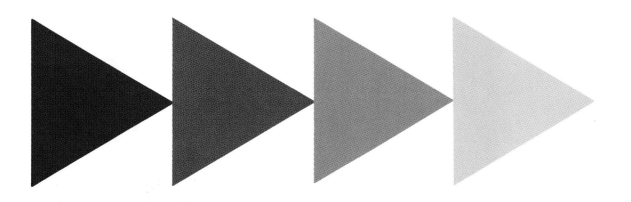

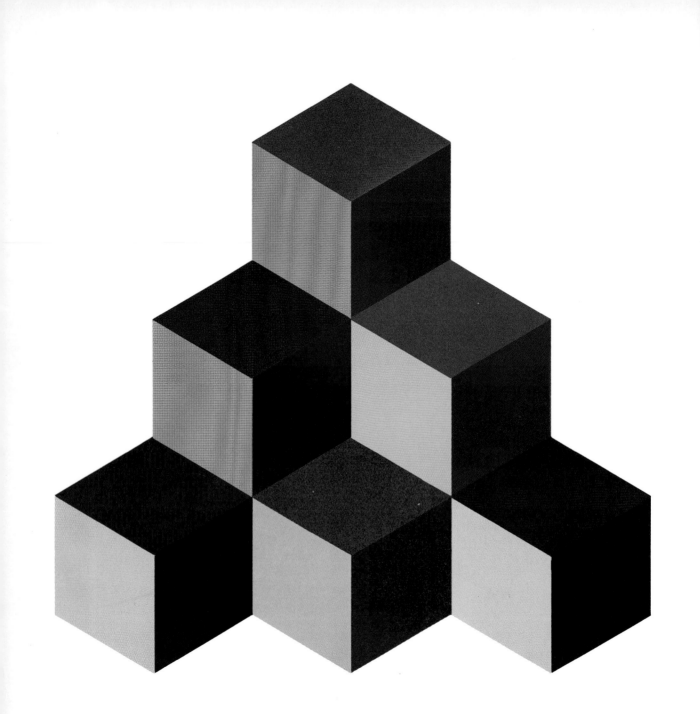

Adding black or white changes any color.

Black darkens a color.

White lightens a color.

Adding gray changes colors, too,

making bright and snappy colors look softer.

Colors play off each other and can fool the eye.
A color is affected by the colors around it.

A dark background makes
a color look lighter than it is.

A light background makes
a color look darker than it is.

A color looks lighter
against black and
darker against white.

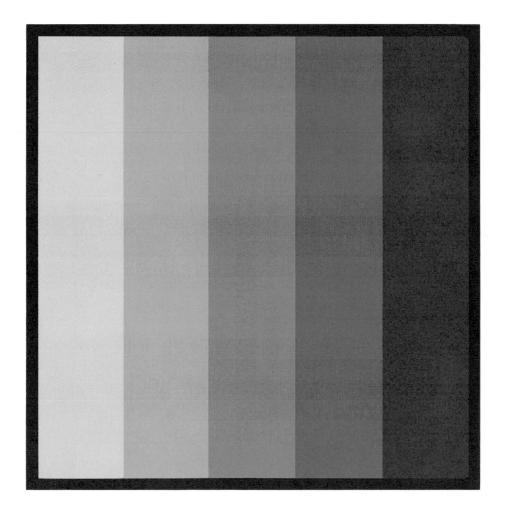

When colors are placed from left to right
in light-to-dark order, the left side of each
color looks darker than the right side.

A bright color comes forward, appearing closer than a soft color, which falls back and seems more distant.

It's no accident that some colors look particularly striking together. Colors directly across from one another on the color wheel are called complementary colors. When two complementary colors are next to each other, both colors look more vibrant than they do alone.

BLUE-GREEN / RED-ORANGE

YELLOW / VIOLET

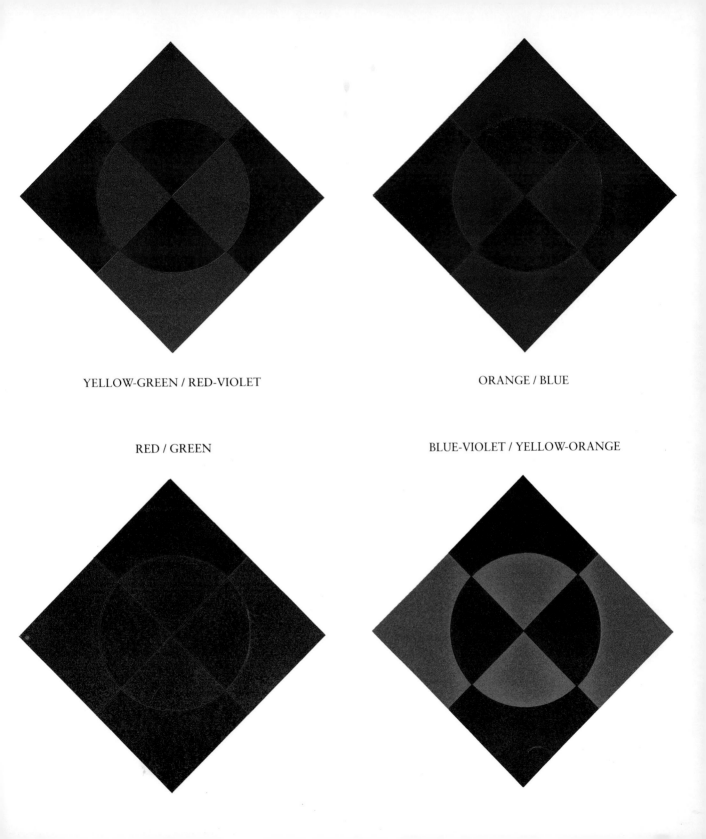

YELLOW-GREEN / RED-VIOLET

ORANGE / BLUE

RED / GREEN

BLUE-VIOLET / YELLOW-ORANGE

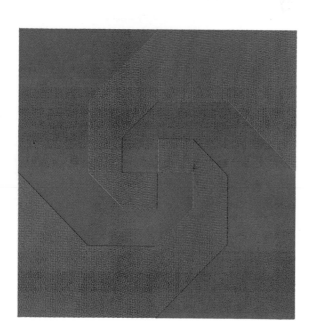

When two colors fill
large areas of equal size,
each color is distinct.

The same colors, placed
in tiny areas of equal size,
tend to blur.

When two colors fill areas of very different sizes,
the color in the smaller area will jump or pop.

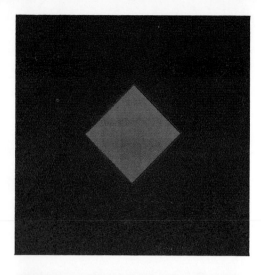

Gray looks different depending on the colors around it. Each background color makes the same gray look different.

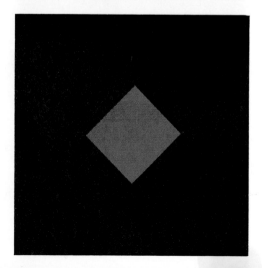

Color can create optical illusions. Only three colors were used in this pattern, but there appear to be more.

Color is everywhere, and everything has color. The variety of color is endless...

and this
is just a
sampler.

The illustrations have been adapted from classic patchwork
quilt patterns. The patterns included, in order of appearance, are:

Wyoming (Jacket)	Diamonds
Pineapple (Title page)	Schoolhouse
Sunflower (Dedication page)	Swallows
Union Square	Center Square
Peony	Ocean Waves
Hexagonal Star	Bars
Star of the East	World Without End
Dresden Plate	Dresden Plate
Fan Quadrille	Vine of Friendship
Pinwheel	Snail Trail
Mowing Machine	Postage Stamp
Wild Goose Chase	Feathered Star
Baby Blocks	Center Diamond
Barn Raising	